IN CHATTER WOOD

JAC JONES

PONT

First Impression – 2004

ISBN 1 84323 290 1

This title is published with the financial support of the
Welsh Books Council.

Printed in Wales at
Gomer Press, Llandysul, Ceredigion

The villagers stood silently in a tense circle, their faces pale, skull-like, in the light of their burning torches. In the centre of the circle was the stone-walled enclosure they had finished building around a dark huddle of trees. The flickering light played on the rough stones, making strange and unsettling shapes in the shadows.

The light also picked out the hunched shape of an old woman. She was performing a weird, heel-stomping dance just outside the wall.

'Is it done, old Sera?' called a voice from the circle.

'HISHT!' she spat, her voice like an angry cat. ''Tis important that it's buried firm in the ground. Its magic will help to hold them here.' She continued stamping the turf with the heels of her dirty bare feet, chanting as she did so.

> 'Stone on stone forever circle,
> Shadow from the light of day,
> Rowan berry, spit of myrtle –
> No evil into goodness stray.'

'Let us be gone from here. I don't trust these doings,' complained another voice from the circle.

'Quiet, fools!' she hissed. 'We are blessed in being given the means to contain them and their evil. Now let me finish!'

Her twig-like fingers clawed out a large pinch of dried leaves and berries from deep within an ancient goatskin

pouch. She shoved them into her mouth and chewed and chewed until dribbles ran down her wrinkled chin. Then, with the torch flames catching the wild bulge of her eyes, she spat over the top of the wall and into the trees.

Out of the walled circle of darkness came a terrible sound – a gabbling, screeching, hair-raising sound, that was both protest and threat. Dropping their torches where they stood, the villagers ran, their wailing and crying becoming one with the chilling howl from the woods.

The old woman also hurried across the cold damp grass, her precious pouch held tight, deep within the black folds of her tattered, crow-flapping cloak.

'Fools! ' she hissed again. 'Will they not see I have made them safe?'

But not once did she look back over her shoulder.

Down in the village, bars were dropped to lock doors securely. On the hill, the torches spluttered out, one by one. And, as the light of the last one died, the now silent gloom within the wall merged into the inky blackness around it.

On a beautiful Autumn Saturday morning, nine hundred and thirty three years later, Ifan Parry chugged along, following a curving furrow, on his clapped-out tractor.

'Damned old wall,' he muttered, wincing, as he heard his potato spinner clip the ancient stone. 'This field's fit only for grazing; that's what it's always been and I should have left it that way.'

Behind him, a team of potato pickers bobbed up and down, busily collecting what the spinner unearthed. Ifan Parry switched off the coughing engine.

'Right!' he shouted. 'Better give this dream machine a rest or it'll go wheels up on me. OK, everybody, let's break for dinner.'

Gwion and Sara straightened out their aching backs and made a place to sit down to eat. Resting themselves against the enclosure wall, they unwrapped their food.

'Oh, no! You're not still on that rabbit food diet?' said Gwion, peering over his twin sister's shoulder as she munched into her lettuce and carrot sandwich. 'Which pop idol do you want to look like this month?'

'Mind your own business, you!' she hissed. 'Just because I don't swallow anything that's thrown my way like you, pedal-bin mouth.'

Gwion grinned as he studied his peanut butter and sausage sandwich.

He enjoyed teasing his sister, almost as much as eating.

'First time I've ever been up this close to Chatter Wood,' he said, looking over his shoulder at the trees behind the wall.

'Well, just you watch out that one of those Red Eyes doesn't nip over and take a bite out of your sandwich,' said one of the adults who had overheard him.

'Red Eyes?' said Gwion, looking puzzled.

'Leave the lad alone,' said one of the others. 'Don't take any notice of him, Gwion Morgan. He just likes to spook people.'

Everybody laughed, except Sara, who was busy digging into the broken soil at her feet.

Later that evening, the twins, their parents and their grandmother, who was visiting, were sitting down to supper.

'Nice potatoes,' said Mam, nodding her approval at the twins.

'Yeah,' said Dad, 'they really hit the spot.'

'The spot they hit is my poor back', winged Gwion, his mouth a tight little circle making a silent 'ouch'.

'Wimp,' scoffed Sara. 'Ifan Parry was a proper Mr Moany today as well,' she continued. 'He kept going on and on that he was going to bulldoze the enclosure and Chatter Wood because it's a pain to go round it.'

'So what?' said Gwion. 'It's dead ugly.'

'Without it, uglier could,' muttered their grandmother, without looking up from her plate.

Everyone stopped eating and looked at her.

'What was that, Gran?' asked Gwion.

'Oh, nothing really,' she said, looking a little embarrassed, 'just something I remember my grandmother reciting to me when I was a little girl.'

'What was that then?' asked Sara.

'Ugly be Chatter Wood. Without it, uglier could . . .' Gran looked at each one in turn and then back to her plate.

'What does that mean?' asked Sara, not entirely sure she wanted to hear the answer.

Gran put down her knife and fork. 'The rhyme was the beginning of a story. Something I remember being told long before I had any hope of understanding what it meant. I always thought it was a kind of warning. It made me uneasy; it was like a burden to carry, but I always knew it was important. My grandmother, Nain Sera Penmynydd – she was your father's great grandmother – she passed it on to me, as her grandmother had passed it to her.'

'But why didn't you tell me about it then, Gran?' asked Sara, looking slightly sulky.

'Naughty, naughty, Grandmother,' said Gwion in a grave voice. 'How do you expect the white witch of the north to save us all, if she doesn't know anything about anything?'

'I should have, but it seems so out of place in today's world, and it's so long ago since I was told the story, I can't remember much . . .' Her voice trailed off, her faded blue eyes looking into Sara's as if searching for the answer. 'But in my bones I feel that it's best to leave Chatter Wood well alone.'

'Spoooooky,' said Gwion. He pulled his jumper up so that his head disappeared and then did a silly walk. 'Lead me to the wooooods,' he said with a ghostly moan, as he walked straight into the kitchen door.

Gwion was reading a football magazine in bed when there was a knock on his door.

'Whoever it is, you can't come in unless you've got three bats and a newt for my cauldron,' he said with a wild cackle.

'You really should be the Professor of Funny at The University of Hilarity,' Sara said, as she settled at the end of his bed.

'Well?' he peered over the top of his magazine.

'Look,' she said, unwrapping something from a piece of her sandwich foil. 'I found it in the potato field today.'

On the Liverpool FC duvet lay a dirty grey stone about the size of a bar of soap.

'Hope that doesn't leave a stain,' he said, picking it up. 'Hey, it's got a little dumpy nude man with a pair of sticky-out ears carved on it!'

'They're not ears, they're horns, pimple-brain. I looked it up on the internet earlier and he's some sort of early charm or something. They used them to ward off evil, sort of protect people, that kind of thing,' said Sara.

'Protect them from what?' asked Gwion, interested despite himself.

'I've just told you: evil. Bad stuff,' she said. 'The net site was called "Shadoworld". It said that charms had been used for thousands of years as a kind of magic against all sorts of nasty things.'

'So what does old horny-head here do then?' asked Gwion.

'He goes back to Celtic times. I think he was called Hu Gadarn, and he was used to control dark forces,' said Sara, solemnly.

'What, like Swamp Thing?' said Gwion, contorting his face into what he thought something green and slimy would look like.

Sara groaned and rolled her eyes.

'So where exactly did you find it?' he asked.

'Sticking out of the earth at the bottom of the enclosure wall where we had our dinner break today.'

'Did you know Liverpool's only three points behind the leaders?' he said, head back in his magazine.

'Well, put candles between my toes and light them,' she said, snatching the stone and stomping along the landing to her bedroom.

Later, in bed, Sara started thinking again about her Gran's mysterious story and her own strange day. Her back ached from all the stooping. She found herself looking for white spots, potato-shaped, in the darkness beneath her lids, and imagined she could feel the stone man still in her hand, cold and heavy. One way or another, Chatter Wood field was still in her mind when, at last, she fell into a restless sleep.

'Uglier could, uglier could,' chattered the voices. The words sounded as if they came from the jaws of dogs, teeth clicking, jowls slobbering. From the dark around her, red points of light watched, unblinking, following her every move. Sara tried to get away but holly bushes and brambles snaked around her, snagging her clothes and flesh, holding her.

'From the wood, uglier could . . .'

The sounds were now in her head, in the leaves, in the shadows between the stones and even in the ground that rippled and heaved beneath her bare feet. Again she tried to get away but her toes became black roots worming into the earth, making her part of Chatter Wood. Through the madness of the undergrowth something crashed its way towards her.

Suddenly there was a blinding light.

'Are you all right, love?' asked her mother, standing at the bedroom door, her finger on the light switch.

'Yes,' said Sara, swallowing hard. 'I am now. Thanks, Mam.'

'Bit of a bad dream, eh? Come on, let's tuck you in.' She lay Sara down from her sitting position and kissed her on the forehead as she plumped up her pillow. 'Hello, what's this?' She pulled the stone man out from beneath the pillow. 'A piece of dirty rock and your lovely clean bedclothes don't go together, do they, Miss? I'll put it here with the rest of your treasures.'

Her mother placed it on the bookcase. 'Goodnight, love,' she said.

A click made it dark. Outside, it was moonless dark, starless dark. Up on the hill, outside the village, Chatter Wood too was dark, apart from the pinpoints of red light that moved about, burning, in the undergrowth.

Next morning, with toast and cereal demolished super-
quick, Sara made her way along the lane towards Chatter
Wood. She didn't want to go up there, especially after last
night, but she felt she just had to, as if something was
calling her. Sitting near the spot where she had dug up the
stone man, she rested against the old wall.

She looked up at the morning sky. The clouds looked like scoops of vanilla ice-cream against the cold blue. It was so lovely, so normal, she began to feel much better about everything. Perhaps last night's bad dream was all to do with an overload of imagination and new potatoes.

She was startled by a loud crashing noise from the other

side of the enclosure of trees. She ran as fast as she could towards the sound of somebody cursing and came to a skidding halt at what she saw. Ifan Parry was beating the bonnet of the tractor with his cap and giving the front wheel a good kicking at the same time. He looked so comical Sara wanted to laugh – until she noticed that the digger bucket had pushed down the wall.

'*You've broken the circle!*' she cried, not quite understanding why she had said such a thing.

He turned around, his face beetroot-red with fury.

'The only thing broken around here is this stupid heap of scrap,' he said, giving the tractor another clout with his cap. 'I can't believe it,' he ranted. 'One little push against that useless wall and the engine blows up. I only had it serviced last night after the potato picking. Cost a fortune. Cash too!'

'You must rebuild the wall, now!' shouted Sara.

'Rebuild it!' he yelled, kicking his cap over the wall. 'I'm trying to knock it all down, girl! Get rid, destroy it. Bulldoze it so flat that even an ant couldn't trip over where it had been. OK? Now scram!'

'But –' Sara started.

'Away!' Ifan Parry said, pointing towards the gate.

She walked away as quickly as she was able over the broken ground, never once looking back over her shoulder. It wasn't that she was afraid of red-faced Ifan Parry; he was a nice man really. What she didn't want to see was the gap in the wall; that made her afraid.

As she turned to close the gate, something caught her eye. It was Ben, Ifan Parry's sheepdog. Ben loved the old farmer. He was always to be seen weaving around his master's legs. Now he sat at the far end of the field, alone, crouching. Watching.

During the break on Monday morning, Sara stood in the middle of the school yard with her best friend, Betsan.

'She broke her leg?' asked Betsan. 'How?'

'She said that she tripped over something on the back lane to Chatter Wood Farm,' answered Sara.

'What was she doing all the way out there?' asked Betsan. 'Your Gran is so ancient, she can hardly walk to the front door.'

'I don't know,' shrugged Sara. 'The doctor at the hospital said she was in shock or something. When she's better she can tell us more.'

'Want another shock?' said Betsan, her voice a whisper.

Sara nodded.

'Well, you know those lovely Shetland ponies at Druid Farm?' She paused, enjoying the drama.

'Yes! Yes!' said Sara impatiently.

'Well, I heard that Wil Henblas found them, totally exhausted, in the lower field on the edge of the marsh. They could hardly stand up and they were covered in froth and some kind of slime. And . . . and,' she said, getting excited, 'there were deep scratches all over their backs, as if they'd been ridden by *something with claws!*'

'*Something . . !*' shrieked Sara, the rest of her words drowned by the school bell.

On their way home, the twins talked breathlessly about all the other stories they had heard in school that day.

'Harry from Morncome Farm said that their prize cockerel was killed during the night,' said Gwion.

'Fox,' said Sara.

'No way,' said Gwion. 'None of the chickens had been touched. That's not the way of the fox, is it? And Harry said that the same thing had happened on two other farms as well.'

'*No cock's-crow, no sunrise,*' said Sara absent-mindedly.

'Why did you say that?' asked Gwion.

'Don't know,' answered Sara, looking embarrassed.

'You're really weird,' said Gwion. 'What's weirder, though, is what happened in the church last night. The place was a mess. The altar-cloth had been ripped to shreds and that big gold cross had been thrown out through the stained-glass window.'

'Crucifix,' said Sara, deep in thought.

'Yeah, yeah,' said Gwion, angry at her interruption. 'What is odd is that they didn't pinch anything. The collection box and the PC and printer in the back room were left alone.'

'Strange,' said Sara. 'Do you know, I've just counted up and that's five different things that happened last night, counting Gran and her broken leg.'

'Oh yes, I nearly forgot. Somebody said that a headstone had been practically dug up in the cemetery of the Wesley Chapel,' said Gwion.

'Six; six. Six things,' she muttered to herself, with a shudder.

When the two arrived home, Gran had returned from hospital. They were so happy to see her surrounded by Get Well cards and flowers. Sara gave her a big hug and a kiss and Gwion scrawled 'Liverpool for ever' on her plaster cast.

That same night, at the end of Chatter Farm lane, dozens of people and children milled around in a choking haze of mist and smoke.

'It's got to be someone from the outside. Nobody from the village would do what's being done to us,' said a voice from deep in an anorak hood. 'Yobs, crazy on drugs, you wait and see.'

'Get a grip, man,' said the twins' father, who had just arrived to see what was going on.

The Vicar's wife greeted him.

'Hello, John. I'm so sorry to hear about your great-grandmother's gravestone being vandalised like that,' she said, her lips trembling. 'With that, and what happened to the church, it's as if we're in some sort of devilish nightmare.'

Several people in the crowd muttered in nervous agreement as they watched the fire brigade leave Chatter Wood Farm.

'The Fire Chief said that the barn and most of the outbuildings are goners,' said Tom Lloyd, who was Ifan Parry's closest neighbour.

'With what's been going on the last couple of nights,' said another voice, 'I'm surprised we're not all goners.'

Sara, in her pyjamas and dressing gown, cuddled up to her gran. She loved Granny-sitting. She had done it before when Gran had had a bad dose of flu.

'I'm glad you've come to spend the night with me, Sara,' Gran said, as they watched the drama of the red sky through the bedroom window of her bungalow.

'I've never seen flames that high except on television,' said Sara.

'Poor, poor, Ifan Parry,' sighed Gran. 'He's always struggled to make a success of Chatter Wood Farm. It was abandoned for years but then he came and took it on. He came here as a young man and he just laughed at all the stories about the farm and old wood.'

'Why did you go up there, Gran?' asked Sara.

'I was just drawn there after our talk. I had a bad feeling. Lots of old tales I was told as a child came back to me.'

Sara snuggled closer. 'Tell me, please,' she said.

'Well,' she began, 'Nain Sera Penmynydd told me that all down the ages people have fallen foul of Chatter Wood. There was one time in the middle ages when they used stones from the wall to repair the church – the parish priest was later found hanging from the yew tree in the cemetery.'

'That's so spooky, Gran. Aren't you supposed to spit when you walk beneath a yew tree?' asked Sara.

'So they say. Then there was the young smithy who fancied clearing the place of evil once and for all. He placed a ring of metal, old horseshoes, around it.'

'Why?'

'Some old belief that metal can protect you from the creatures of the otherworld. Soon after, all the horses he shod either took sick or stumbled and broke a leg. Farmers from all around stopped using him and he died a broken man, and all because of Chatter Wood.'

'Why is it called Chatter Wood?' asked Sara.

'It's been said that, sometimes, in the dead of night, you can hear sounds inside the walls, like a sinister chattering,' she said.

Sara's eyes were like blue fire. 'Has anyone ever seen anything?' she whispered.

'Yes,' said Gran, looking out of the window at the moon needling its cold light through the wood in the distance. 'There is a story of a local man who did. Dic Ferret he was called. Famous round here as a poacher and a bit of a drunkard. One night, long ago, he was out ferreting, and he took shelter from a storm in Chatter Wood. He fell asleep there and when he woke up he could hardly breathe, there was such a terrible stench.'

'Urgh,' croaked Sara, her hand to her mouth.

'The local legend was that he told his minister every

detail. He said to him, "They were all around, shadowy shapes, lurking, watching. They stared at me with eyes the colour of blood and forced me to remember all the bad things in my life. Nothing good, only bad." Well, that's the story, anyway.'

'What happened to Dic Ferret, Gran?' asked Sara.

'They say he became a recluse: did no more poaching but a lot more drinking,' she answered. 'Then one day, he disappeared; some say he was "taken". Anyway, he was never seen again.'

'But who exactly took him, Gran?' persisted Sara.

'The old folk, long ago, had a name for them: they called them the "Tylwyth Tywyll". That's Welsh for the *dark tribe.*'

Sara shuddered.

'They were creatures of the dark, all right. Fed off evil and poisoned good. But then, hundreds of years ago, legend says, they were penned up by spellmakers, so that decent people could get on with their lives.'

'Penned up!' squeaked Sara, clutching the bed sheet to her face. 'In Chatter Wood?'

'Yes, and other places like it all over the land. They can't do any harm in there. We should be safe from them – unless they're set loose, of course.'

Sara's heart sank. She almost knew what her grandmother would say next.

'And they were loose when you got there, Gran?'

'Oh yes, and they knew very well who I was,' she said,

pointing to her broken leg. 'The one thing I can't understand is, why they are amongst us.'

'I think I know, Gran,' said Sara nervously.

She fetched the stone man, described where she had found it, and told Gran the story about Ifan Parry and his digger as well. How he had breached the enclosure wall. She realised now why this had made her feel so scared.

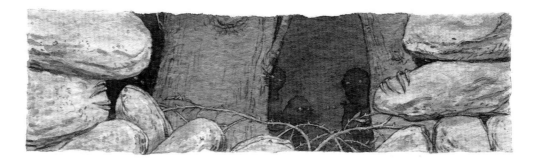

All Gran could say was, 'Oh, Sara fach!'

They were silent for a while and then Sara turned very slowly and looked at her grandmother.

'Is now the time of "uglier could", Gran?'

'I afraid it is, my lovely,' she replied, touching her grand-daughter's cheek. 'I'm also afraid that what happens next will be up to you. Now go to the old chest over there and under the blankets you'll find a little cask, an ancient cask. Bring it to me.'

Sara watched her Gran run her fingers back and forth along the edges of the curiously patterned lid until, with the slightest of groans, it opened.

A thin finger and thumb dipped into the cask and emerged, holding a wrinkled leather pouch.

'Do you know what this contains?' asked Gran. With trembling fingers, she placed the pouch on to the steady hand of her grand-daughter.

'The answer?' said Sara, her eyes burning with the same ancient light as her grandmother's.

'I hope so, cariad. I was never called upon to open it. That is until now, and being the useless thing that I am, I have to pass the duty on to you.'

'I feel scared,' said Sara.

'Come on, come here and snuggle up, I have other things to tell you. Things you'll need to know,' said Gran.

Sara and her grandmother talked late into the night. At last they fell asleep, exhausted.

Up on the hill, just before sunrise, shadowy shapes scuttled back through the gap in the wall, their red eyes beacons of evil. Apart from the distant scream of a fox, the only sound to be heard was the chatter of wet mouths.

The next morning, after coming home from Gran's house, Sara cornered Gwion in his bedroom and insisted that he listen to what she had to say. Sara told him part of Gran's story, but kept the scarier bits to herself. Perhaps she'd tell him later, she thought. After the task was done.

At first he kept interrupting her with 'No way', 'rubbish' and 'gross' but then he became quiet. Pale-faced, he sat on the end of his bed and let her finish her story.

'Gran told me this was something only I could do,' she said. 'She also said, the last time this same thing had to be done, our great-great-grandmother was the one who had to do it.'

'The one you were named after,' said Gwion. 'Nain Sera Penmynydd.'

'How did you know?' asked Sara.

'I overheard Dad talking about her and something that had happened to her gravestone,' said Gwion. 'He was really wound up, too.'

'He's not the only one,' Sara muttered to herself. 'Right, we'll have to go and do it this afternoon. Straight after school, OK?'

'What do you mean, *we?*'

'You're allowed to help me because you're my twin,' she said as she spun on her heel.

'No, *you're my twin*,' Gwion hissed through gritted teeth, flopping back on to the bed. 'I was born first. And, by three minutes and forty five seconds too. A mile can be run in that time,' he muttered, as he reached for a football magazine.

Straight after tea they slipped away unnoticed, except by Gran. She watched them, from behind the lace curtains, running up the lane. She knew where they were going. Her hands, the colour of white wax candles, gripped each other tightly, as if in prayer. She had to be strong for Sara. She found herself chanting.

'Stone on stone forever circle,
Shadow from the light of day,
Rowan berry, spit of myrtle –
No evil into goodness stray.'

Only when she'd finished did it dawn on her that she had no memory of having heard those words before. Her hands gripped even tighter.

Soon, the twins were making their way across the potato field toward Chatter Wood.

'Do they know we're coming?' whispered Gwion nervously.

'Oh, yes,' whispered Sara. 'Gran said they would and that they would also know what we're here to do. It's happened to them before by the ones who know the verse.'

'But why do they return to the woods? Why don't they escape?'

'They move on only when there is nothing left to spoil,' answered Sara, her voice low and strangely hollow.

Gwion stopped in his tracks and stared at his sister, his head cocked to one side.

'Who told you that, Sara?'

'No one. I just know. OK?' she scolded, taking her anger out on a small, rejected potato with an almighty kick.

Gwion forgot the tension for a moment and followed the flight of the potato. 'Wow! Respect, sis,' he said.

'Don't even think about it. One word about football and you'll follow the potato. OK?'

They continued over the broken earth in silence, until they arrived at the foot of the wall.

'They'll try to stop us,' said Gwion, his voice rising. 'I'm scared!'

'HISHT!' said Sara. 'We've got the stone charm and besides, they're things of the dark, not daylight. So we have to take a chance.'

They stood and looked at the tumbled stones where Ifan Parry's tractor had begun the whole thing. Neither of the twins ventured beyond the gap in the wall.

'Poo,' said Gwion, holding his nose. 'What's that stink?'

'A dead rat, or something,' said Sara, not daring to tell him about the story Gran had told her. 'Come on, Gwion, let's get going.'

She stooped to pick up one of the moss-covered stones. 'Gurg,' she gasped, 'I can't budge it.'

'Girlie!' sneered Gwion, brushing her to one side. 'Let me at it.'

His face was an unnatural purple colour before he conceded, falling on his backside. 'It's as if it's stuck to the ground!'

They tried several other smaller stones, but every time it was the same.

'That smell,' said Gwion, 'it's getting worse. It's making me gag.'

'It's Them! The stones, the stench. They're trying to stop us,' gasped Sara. 'Look, the sun, it'll be set in less than half an hour! We have to get lucky, and quick!'

'The lumpy dumpy lucky man!' yelled Gwion, his body rigid with fear.

'What are you on about?' Sara's voice went from scream to whisper in five words.

'Bury the stone man!' he said, pointing a trembling finger at the ground. 'Quick, Sara!'

In no time at all, they had dug a deep hole in the broken soil, dropped the stone man in and covered it up.

Gwion picked up a large stone now as if it were a beach ball.

'Look! See!' he said. 'And the stink's gone too.'

'Brill, Gwion. You're a genius,' said Sara. 'Now the wall.'

They worked quickly and in silence. Their child-thin arms lifted and arranged the large and ancient stones as if by magic. Stone after stone found its rightful place. Then it was done.

Neither could believe that they had finished the task so easily, but they had.

'Rock on rock!' shouted a relieved Gwion. 'Just look at that, you can hardly tell where the gap was!' He did a mad March Hare dance, hopping around in ever-decreasing circles.

'Right,' said Sara, taking no notice of her brother, and going back to the place where they had buried the horned man, *'tis important that it's buried firm in the ground.'* She removed her shoes and stamped the earth flat with her heels.

'Now the pouch to complete the Answer,' she whispered to herself, rooting around in her pockets, chanting as she did so. She emptied some of the strange mixture of dried-up berries and leaves into her hand. Gwion looked on in disgust as she took a mouthful and started to chew like a frantic rabbit.

'Urgh! Gross! Not only do you eat bunny food, you're beginning to look like one,' he said, putting his hands on top of his head and waggling them back and forth. 'I think you're losing it, Sara.'

'It's shpart of the shpell,' she spluttered from a full mouth, with dribble running down her chin.

As Gwion yelled 'Shpell?' she spat over the wall.

Suddenly, the twins bent double, hands pressed hard to

their ears. Rooks and crows rose, scattering like black confetti. Sheep, frantic with fear, left clumps of themselves in the brutal blackthorn as they fled from the terrible sounds that came from Chatter Wood.

Then came the quiet. A quiet that was a hiss in the head until the ears popped and made it pure.

'It's OK, now, Gwion,' Sara said, gradually straightening up.

He lay on the ground, hands still on his ears, flatter than a cow pat.

'GWION!'

Eyes still closed tight, he rolled over on his back.

'Is it all over?' he asked, his voice just a squeak.

'Yes,' said another voice.

The twins nearly leapt out of their skins.

'I heard what I heard. And now I know what I think I've always known, but I chose to ignore it. You've closed the circle, haven't you, Sara?' said Ifan Parry.

Sara, wide-eyed, struggled to say something.

'It's all right, girl. We understand now, don't we, Ben?' he said, patting the tail-wagging dog at his heels. 'We can all go home now,' he smiled.

The twins had never ever seen him smile before.

The three of them, and a bounding Ben, walked towards the field gate and the setting sun.

Then they were gone.

Now there was only the rustle of a robin's excitement as it rooted around for grubs in the disturbed soil outside the wall. Then, as the light died, a dreadful, angry, slobbering chatter rose from within the enclosure. A gabble of *almost words* from the trapped. The robin flew away, startled. Its breast was the same colour as the terrible blood-red eyes that watched it go.

That night, in the freezing cold, small hours, a barn owl studied the figures standing in a silent circle around Chatter Wood. Its large night eyes reflected the eerie blue light of their burning torches and their pale skull-like faces. Some time later, satisfied, they turned away and, in single file, followed the hunched figure of an old woman into the mist.

The owl watched them go, and as the last light blinked out, it took to the air like a whisper.

The village enjoyed a deep and peaceful sleep that night, to wake up to an unusually early frost. Ifan Parry tinkered with his tractor, grateful that his potato-sacks were safely stored in the barn. Gran, rested and chirpy, switched on the kettle and arranged three mugs ready. The twins, excited, shot out of the house into a world made clean and new by the white blanket that covered it.

'If the weather carries on like this, I think I'll ask Santa for a pack of huskies this Christmas,' said Gwion.

'You're mad,' said Sara. 'Race you to Gran's house.'

In no time at all they were both laughing dots in the distance, at the end of their own footprints.